NICKI WEISS

The World Turns Round and Round

SCHOLASTIC INC.

New York   Toronto   London   Auckland   Sydney
Mexico City   New Delhi   Hong Kong   Buenos Aires

ISBN 0-439-38903-8

12 11 10 9 8 7 6 5   3 4 5 6 7/0

Printed in the U.S.A.   24

First Scholastic printing, February 2002

Colored pencils were used for the full-color art.

The text type is Futura BT.

For David

What was sent to the brown-eyed boy
From his abuela in Mexico?

From Tapalpa came a sombrero of straw.
Oh, he never saw
Such a sombrero of straw
From rural Mexico.

What was sent to the pigtailed girl
From her aunt in Colorado?

FOURTH CLASS

FOURTH CLASS

From Durango came cowboy boots of blue.
So shiny and new,
Those cowboy boots of blue
From the mountains of Colorado.

What was sent to the boy with curls
From his mjomba in Kenya?

From Nairobi came a dashiki so grand.
He was proud to stand
In that dashiki so grand
From Kenya on the African plain.

What was sent to the black-haired girl
From her ojisan in Japan?

From Kyoto came a kimono of green.
How she felt like a queen
In that kimono of green
From Japan far over the sea.

What was sent to the red-haired boy
From his babushka in Russia?

From Moscow came a shapka, a hat.
How it pleased him,
That little furry hat
From the far-off Russian land.

The world turns round and round.

What was sent to the longhaired girl
From her chachi in India?

From Agra came a sari to wear.
Made of silk so rare,
That sari to wear
From sultry India.

What was sent to the freckled boy
From his uncle up in Maine?

From Portland came some mittens of wool.
They felt wonderful,
Those knitted mittens of wool
From the rocky shores of Maine.

What was sent to the girl with braids
From her jidd in Egypt?

From Cairo came a kaffiyeh of white.
It gave such delight,
That kaffiyeh of white
From Egypt in the desert sun.

What was sent to the smiling twins
From their ba in Vietnam?

From Can Tho came some dep in twos.
How they loved those shoes,
Those little thongs in twos
From the jungles of Vietnam.

What was sent to the lucky girl
From her tante on the Haitian isle?

From Port-au-Prince came a chemise aux fleurs.
How it flattered her,
That chemise aux fleurs
From Haiti, island of green.

The world turns round and round.

But it's really not so far,

Not so far from there to here.

Kaffiyeh, sari, dep in pairs—
Dashiki, shapka, mittens to wear.

We're part of here and part of there,
And the world turns round and round.

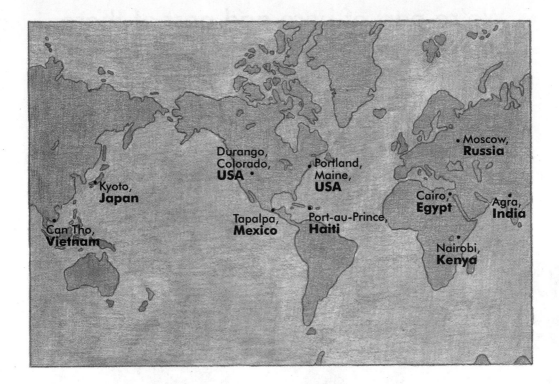

THE RELATIVES

Abuela (ah-BWEL-ah) means *grandmother* in Spanish.
Mjomba (mah-JOM-bah) means *uncle* in Swahili.
Ojisan (o-JEE-san) means *grandfather* in Japanese.
Babushka (BAH-boosh-kuh) means *grandmother* in Russian.
Chachi (cha-CHEE) means *aunt* in Hindi.
Jidd (jid) means *grandfather* in Arabic.
Ba (bah) means *grandmother* in Vietnamese.
Tante (tahnt) means *aunt* in French.

THE PRESENTS

sombrero (som-BRER-o)
dashiki (dah-SHEE-kee)
kimono (ki-MO-no)
shapka (SHAP-kah)
sari (SAH-ree)
kaffiyeh (kuh-FEE-yah)
dep (zep)
chemise aux fleurs (sheh-MEEZ o fluhr)